Written, Directed and Produced by
Christopher Robertson

Cover art by Matt Taylor IG: @art.by.theshrimpshackslasher

Also Available

Virgin Night
My Zombie Sweetheart
The October Society - Season One

Candy Apple Smiles (featured in Blood Rites Horror Welcome to the Funhouse)

Coming soon…
The Cotton Candy Massacre
The October Society - Season Two

Warning!

The Following Contains Scenes of Explicit Clownage, Violence, and Gore.

Discretion is Advised.

Goons and Grease Paint

Bonkin's Bonanza.

Sometime in the early 70s.

Fade in: on a match, sparking against a rough, dirt-ringed nail. Shadows shimmy across the kid's face. Let's say kid 'cause even with the beaten leather jacket, collar turned up, and a few days of stubble on his chin, he barely looks old enough to drive the '57 Fairlane cooling in the dirt. He parks his ass on the hood.

Ain't his car; ain't even his jacket, even if it does fit just right. He found it in the backseat when he boosted the car earlier that afternoon.

No way the man's gonna catch him around the back of the carnival, and not just 'cause the road's off-limits to the public. Cops don't come around Bonkin's, not unless it's to pick up their take. Still, he fidgets nervously, lighting up yet another smoke and fixing the collar on his jacket for the fifth or sixth time.

"Jesus Christ, Bailey, hurry the fuck up." The cigarette bounces with every word. The kid's on edge; no two ways about it.

Though the car radio's real low, he can hear Derek and the Dominoes singing about some girl called Layla putting them on their knees, and he thinks, damn you too, huh?

He spots a shape heading towards the back gate. She's all messed up blonde feathered waves, denim cut-offs, and knee-high boots.

"Finally."

He flicks the cigarette into the pile with the rest, a small smoldering monument to his wasted time.

Bailey gives a wave that makes her crop-top rise up, and he can almost hear the clattering of the tasseled beads.

He's about to wave back when he sees it wasn't meant for him.

The kid on the hood of the Fairlane spits.

"Perry."

A big guy steps out of the booth by the back gate, the kind of heavy you can't tell if it's fat or muscle but does it really matter when it hits like a dump truck all the same? The kid's jaw still hurts from the one and only time he dared tell the oaf to keep his gorilla hands off his girl.

Perry eyes Bailey up and down, not giving two shits that her ride's waiting.

Bailey flirts with the goon, giggling at whatever he says, batting hands and eyes at him. She lets the big guy goose her ass, pull her in close, and only wiggles out in a playful, maybe next time, kinda way.

It annoys the shit out of him, watching Bailey work the guard over like that. He knows the kind of work she does in the backyard of Bonkin's Bonanza, he's no fool, but he doesn't need to see it. 'Least when he's at home or bagging groceries at K-Mart, he can imagine it's just a job. She's gotta act like she enjoys it, same as he's gotta smile for the shitheels who don't want their meat touching their apples. That doesn't mean he's gotta like it, though. That he's gotta like the thought of Perry's meat slapping against Bailey's apples. Or why she's gotta do it for the big goon. Bonko doesn't seem like the type to let any of his crew get a free taste, but Perry's pawing at Bailey like he owns her - and she ain't doing a damn thing about it.

It's all he can think about, even as she saunters over to the boosted car with a smile on her face and a loud "Baby!" on her lips.

"The hell was all that?"

"Baby?"

"Why you gotta let that goon feel you up like that?"

"Munroe, Baby, it's just an act."

She leans in and tries to plant a kiss on Munroe's cheek. Doesn't matter if she brushes her teeth or swills a half-bottle of Williamson's Shine - he doesn't like her kissing him after she puts in a shift. Swears he can feel the other men's gunk crawling across his teeth. He turns away.

"I thought you was down with it? 'Sides," she leans in real close, whispering in his ear, "had to make sure the dummy knew I had nothin' on me for when shit hits the fan."

"Whatever." Munroe pushes her off, and yanks open the car door.

"Nice ride, boosted?" Bailey climbs in the other side.

"You ever let him fuck you?" Munroe can't get past it.

"This ain't the time, Baby, we gotta-"

"I ain't going anywhere till you answer." Munroe kills the engine.

"Baby, don't do this."

Bailey glances toward the backyard. It's all quiet for now, but she knows the shit's about to hit the fan, and the last place she wants to be is downwind.

"Did you ever let that big, greasy goon stick it in you?"

"Baby, please just drive."

Munroe pulls the keys out and makes a show of closing his fist around them.

Bailey sighs. "He paid so-"

"Fuck!" Munroe slams down on the wheel and forces himself not to throw up. He can live with the thought of heaving bodies on top of his girl, long as he can't put a face to them, but now all Munroe can picture is Perry's self-satisfied sneer staring right at him while he crushes Bailey below that pale, hairy monster gut.

He starts the car back up and drives in silence. Bailey tries to stroke his arm, and Munroe just pulls away. She figures she'll leave him be for a while; he gets like this sometimes when he thinks too much about the work she does - did. Bailey tells herself, work I did, 'cause they'll never see this damn place again after tonight.

Instead of taking the road back to the highway, Munroe swings around and pulls the car up around the front. It's nearly closing time at Bonkin's Bonanza, and those still left in the carnival drip out the front gate. Parents carry sugar-crashed kids in their arms between the clown's giant fiberglass legs that make up the front gate. One of the lights inside his gawking eyes has gone out, making the freaky thing look like it's had a stroke.

Munroe kills the engine and settles in to wait.

"You know I love you, right?" Bailey finally speaks, focusing on her twiddling fingers instead of Munroe's scowl.

"I know," Munroe sighs. "It just ain't easy, thinkin' 'bout you doing that stuff."

"Well, you don't gotta no more, right?" Bailey puts her hand on his arm and smiles when he doesn't pull away. "Soon as - hey, there he is!" Bailey points towards the front gate.

"Jesus, be cool!"

"Nobody's watchin' us out here, Baby. Give him the sign."

Munroe flashes the lights three times quickly, and a small boy with a plastic clown mask makes his way over to the car. A heavy backpack sags down, hanging too low against his back.

Bailey's buzzing as she leans into the back and opens one of the doors. The kid in the clown mask climbs in, struggling to take the backpack off before dumping it on the floor - it lands with a heavy thud and rattle.

"Come give Mommy a hug!" Bailey leans through, butt wedged in the gap between seats, and doesn't care she's flashing anyone who walks by.

"Jesus, Bailey," Munroe grumbles. "You're givin' everyone a free show."

"Aren't you Mommy's good boy!" Bailey squeezes the kid as Munroe starts the car.

Creedence is singing about seeing the rain on the radio, and the road's blocked by the time they get turned around. A whole bunch of cars, all trying to force their way through the exit from three different directions, turn the road into a jumble of rattling exhausts and blaring horns.

"I don't like this." Bailey shifts nervously. "They're gonna know it's gone before we even get out of the parking lot."

"So what?" Munroe tries to move up and gets cut off. He throws a suburban-looking dad the bird. "Like you said, they know you didn't take it. It's all copacetic."

"Still. Take the back road, Baby. Sitting here's making me bug out for real."

"Fine." Munroe groans and turns the car around. He has to go up on the grass to head back and feels confused stares from everyone waiting in line. The back road's more of a trail than anything. Not worth driving if you care about your car. It's just for backyard business, or so Munroe was warned. He doesn't care about that, but Bailey was as serious as it gets about not pissing off her boss. Feels kinda right to take the freaky clown's private road out, with an entire weekend's worth of backyard take tucked away inside that rucksack. They don't have time to count it right now, but if Bailey wasn't bullshitting about how much money goes through Bonkin's, they're gonna be sitting pretty for a real long time.

They barely make it a few yards down the overgrown road, gnarled branches scratching the car's paint to shit when they're stopped. The headlights land on something pale and white, a wall of it - and an assortment of bright hues laughing silently in the dark.

"Fuck!" Munroe slams on the brakes.

"Shit-shit-shit!" Bailey panics and starts looking around desperately. "He knows, Bonko knows!"

On the road in front of them stands a line of pissed-off clowns. Tall ones, short ones, skinny and hefty - all giving the car mean stares, with meaner things in their hands. Chains, mallets, hatchets, and picks.

Munroe flips it to reverse and leans over his seat. The kid in the back starts to wail.

"Can you shut him the fuck up! I need to concentrate!" Munroe yells.

Bailey's in full-on panic mode. She clutches her heart, dirty-blonde hair swishing around as she looks for a way out.

"Shit!"

Munro comes to another line of armed clowns, blocking the road back. One of them, a tall and freakishly skinny sad face in a porkpie hat, levels a revolver at the car - the threat brings Munroe to a dead stop.

"What are we gonna-"

The driver-side window explodes as a meaty fist shatters through. It grabs Munroe by the hair, and he has just enough time to see Perry and that fucking sneer before the goon slams Munroe's head on the wheel.

Cut to: black.

Fade in: on stubby fingers, sliding across a shelf packed tight with records. They stop, tapping one with a giggle.

A needle's point hovers over black vinyl, carefully lowered into a well-worn groove. Static crackles as the record spins, and a single guitar stroke strums through the speaker.

Roy Orbinson croons about a candy-colored clown they call the Sandman.

He faces the record player, back to a grand office adorned with framed posters for all sorts of carnival acts, like Chet Redwood the Strongest Man Alive and Marianna, the Magnificent Fortune Teller.

The little man waves his arms to the music. Not much higher than the shelf the speakers rest on - barely four feet tall if we're not counting the shocks of hair sticking up on either side of his otherwise bald head. Like a troll doll some kid messed up with a broken razor.

The little man cavorts with a jumping heel click and props himself down in front of a vanity mirror easily twice his size. He sings along with Roy as he dabs a dirty brush in an open tin of white power.

"I close my eyes-"

"Boss!" The door clangs open, and a roustabout barges in. "We got a-"

"What did I say about comin' in here when I don't gots my f-f-f-face on!?" The little man screams, sounding like a pissed-off tea kettle.

The roustabout seizes up. "I, uh, didn't, I'm-"

"Shut the f-f-f-fuckin' door, or I'll shut it on your f-f-f-fuckin' head."

"S-sorry, boss." The roustabout quickly backs out of the room, head bowed with flop sweat dripping to hypnotically mismatched black and white tiles.

The little man goes about his work as the music washes away the bad taste of the interruption.

He slathers his face and neck with grease paint, leaving behind smears across his shirt and collarbone. It covers his face and ears, reaching as far as the edge of his forehead in uneven, sloppy dashes of pale white. Some of it catches on the myriad of pocked scars that make it pointless for him to let his hair grow. He uses some blue to paint streaks down through his eyes and then twists some of it onto the jutting hair on either side.

Next comes some red, which he takes in two hands and covers his cheeks and chin - turning the bottom third of his face crimson. It catches on stubble and glides over flaky lips.

The clown looks at himself in the mirror and smiles through yellow-black teeth that reek of moonshine as he pops on a red, round nose. He giggles and honks it as his eyes wander to the reflection of an unconscious girl. She seems dead to the world, but an occasional blink shows she's still alive—a needle in her arm and underwear on the floor as she reclines on a stained loveseat.

"Sorry, Toots. Daddy's gots work to do, ay-yup!"

Cut to: Munroe waking with what he thinks is the worst hangover in the world. He's gotta still be drunk, though, 'cause the room feels like it's spinning. None of the walls seem like they're the same size. Same with the tiles on the floor. There's nothing else. It might have been a bathroom or larder at some point - it has that kind of persistent chill. There are no windows, just empty picture frames hanging below a bare bulb and over a big, rusty drain on the floor.

Aside from the ringing in his head, he hears something like a wounded puppy crying for help. It's no dog, though; it's his girl. Bailey's bound and gagged, with her eyes about to burst out of her skull.

"The hell-"

"Shut it." Perry whacks Munroe over the head again, and the evening's misadventure comes crashing into place as the goon grabs a fistful of his long, greasy hair.

"Watchit," a nasal voice warns. "Bonko ain't gon' like you breakin' what's his."

Munroe feels the shudder surge through Perry like a shock of pure ice. The goon's meaty fingers tense up and let go without another word.

Wincing, Munroe looks over his shoulder, and aside from the goon himself, there are a few of those carnie clowns, still armed but just keeping watch.

A few questions come to mind - like, since when did Blinky and Bozo go all Butch and Sundance? How did this Bonko teach a shaved ape to speak, and why are they still alive? Everything Bailey's said about the boss clown makes him sound like the meanest son of a bitch who ever lived, and if he's scary enough to put the fear into a goon like Perry, he must be something else. All things considered, Munroe would prefer a bullet to the head than to find out what makes both his girl and that mountain of meat tremble.

A set of metal doors clang open on that thought, and though light streams in from the outside, Munroe can't make out who's entering. He hears them, shoes clicking on the tiles, but whoever's come in can't be seen over the line of carnie clowns keeping watch.

For a second, Munroe relaxes. He can't be the big guy, probably some other lackey or-

"Here dey is, boss," Perry says.

Munroe gulps. He looks straight down, not that it'll do much, but maybe if he shows enough respect and contrition, he'll crawl out of this with a few broken bones and missing teeth.

A pair of too-long, mismatched shoes come to stand before his bowed head.

"Eyes up here, f-f-f-fuckwit." His voice makes Munroe think of a TV gangster caught huffing paint fumes. He follows a pair of short legs up dirty, patched slacks, then across a stained once-white work shirt and garishly colorful suspenders. As Munroe sets eyes on the little clown's face, any hope he had of contrition goes out the window. One look at the severe steely glare in the tiny man's eyes is all it takes to send Munroe into a fit of hysterical laughter.

Bailey whines, screaming into her gag as her eyes plead with Munroe to stop.

"Alright, jokes on me. Send in the real boss."

"You think I'm f-f-f-foolin' around?" The little clown smiles so wide his red-painted jaw reaches his eyes. He leans over, hands behind his back, till his round nose is an inch from Munroe's.

"I'm thinking-"

Bonko swings a ball-peen hammer around, catching Munroe's chin with the back end. The blow sends three teeth through the air with a jet of blood, and Munroe hits the tiles before the teeth skitter across the room.

Bailey's muffled screams catch Bonko's attention. He leaves Munroe spitting blood on the floor and jauntily hops over to her.

"Bailey.
Bailey-Bailey-Bailey-Bailey-Bailey." Bonko hooks the gag and rips it from her face. "You've been a naughty girl."

"I didn't mean it! I swear, Bonko! It was his idea-"

Munroe tries to protest, but all that comes out are sobbing, agonized muffles, and bloody spit bubbles.

Bonko draws in a breath, chuckling like a gasping hyena.

"You mean you was just bein' a good girl, and this," Bonko growls, "piece of shit!" He kicks Munroe square in the gut. "Somehow knew where the take was?" Bonko gets right back in Bailey's face so fast she yelps. "Huh!?"

"No, I mean, I didn't-"

"Shove it!" Bonko snarls so bad his gums begin to bleed. He lets her see it, writhe in the magnitude of her situation. "One of yous is takin' a trip to Bruce-"

"No! Please!"

Bonko backhands her, knocking Bailey to the ground and lighting what's left of Munroe's dignity on fire. It's more instinct than anything, and it gives him the strength to go at the clown.

He skids to a halt as Bonko holds the hammer aloft.

"You think you're a big man? Huh? What kinda man uses his woman to rip off a score?" Bonko fake-outs with the hammer, making Munroe flinch. "What kinda man lets his woman f-f-f-fuck for a livin'?"

Munroe spits a glob of gore on the floor in defiance.

"Let's play a game." Bonko puts both hands behind his back. "Pick a hand. You choose the empty one, and it's your bitch I send to Brucie."

"Please, Bonko!" Bailey begs.

"Pick the hammer," Bonko chuckles, "and you'll get smashed! Ay-yup!"

Munroe looks at the gang of stone-faced clowns behind Bonko. The only one not in grease paint is the lumbering Perry, who's pale enough as is and somehow looks dumber than all the other bozos combined. Whether or not Bonko's for real, it's not like he has a hell of a lot of choices. Munroe nods, agreeing to Bonko's terms. Fifty-fifty shot of getting out of here, that's better odds than he'd expected - even if it means

Bailey's the one who pays. It's her fault, anyway. She told him about the money. He wasn't serious when he came up with the idea. It was just a joke, saying how the kid could smuggle it out without suspicion. She's the one who actually did it, put that shit in their son's bag. All Munroe did was boost a car and give her a lift.

"Pick." Bonko grins right into Munroe's trembling face. "Don't cha trust me? Don't cha think Bonko plays fair?"

Munroe's jaw sits loose, a stream of pinkish drool running down an off-angle chin, and he considers.

"No," Bailey pleads, cowering on the floor.

Munroe lifts one shaky arm, finger outstretched, and hesitates before pointing to the left. He shuts his eyes, squeezes them tight, and waits for what's to come.

Nothing.

Munroe cracks one eye, then the other, and looks from Bonko's leering smirk to an empty, outstretched hand. So much relief floods Munroe's system that it washes away the pain. He feels his soul lift just as Bonko brings the hammer around and takes out his knee with an echoing, stomach-turning crack.

"Don't cha know?" Bonko screams. "Ain't no such thing as fair at the carnival."

Munroe crawls backward, dragging one leg that sits all wrong and leaving a trail of blood across the wonky tiles.

Bonko advances, twirling the hammer in his hand.

Munroe backs up to a wall and holds his hands out as a pathetic last-ditch defense. "Please," he begs with a broken jaw.

"No!" A kid screams as he barges into the room, small and fast enough to weave through the guards and get between Bonko and Munroe.

Bonko finds himself staring at his own face for a second - a cheap, plastic mirror image held across the kid's head with a raggedy string.

"Please don't hurt my daddy!" The kid begs, holding his arms out to make himself as big as possible.

Bonko flits back and forth between Perry and the kid. Holding a finger at the boy, he asks, "Who's the wiener weasel?"

"He was in the car." Perry shrugs like that's an answer.

"Sorry, Bonko!" One of the Coochie Trailer girls, sweaty and out of breath, comes through the door. "He got away."

"Please." The kid snivels beneath his mask. "I'm sorry for what I did."

"F-f-f-for what you did?" Bonko tilts his head. "Kiddo, you best start tellin' ol' Bonko the toot-tootin' truth 'f-f-f-fore I smash it outta ya."

"No!" Bailey scrambles toward them and freezes as Bonko flexes his hammer wrist.

"Promise you won't hurt my mommy and daddy no more?"

"Kiddo, I promise I will f-f-f-fuck them up unless-"

"No!" The kid begins to cry but pushes it down. "Mommy put somethin' in my backpack and told me not to take it off and not to open it. She said it was a surprise for daddy, and I was to look after it until she was done with work."

"That a f-f-f-fact?" Bonko's lips curl as he looks at Bailey. He closes the distance between himself and the kid, then leans over slightly so they're face to face. "See these scars, kiddo?" Bonko runs a bloody hand over his rough head. Calloused skin catches on stubble and explores uneven lumps of scar tissue. "My pops gave these to me."

The kid simpers.

"LOOK AT ME!" Bonko roars, and as much as the kid jumps, he holds his ground. Snatching one of his hands, Bonko forces the boy to touch his scars. "My pops was an ugly man on the inside, so he made me one on the outside. For years I hated what I saw in the mirror. But ya know what I learned when I grew up?"

The kid shakes his head.

"We're not our f-f-f-folk's f-f-f-fuck-ups." Bonko smiles. "And that's the toot-tootin' truth."

As Bonko lets go of the kid's hand, one of the strings on the mask pops free. It falls to the floor, plastic echoing on tiles.

"Well, would ya look at that?"

The boy before Bonko can't be more than ten, but he has a face full of long, scraggly hair that hangs down from mutton chops that are almost the size of his face.

"You're something, ain'tcha? What's your name, kiddo?"

"Weese," Munroe answers for him, hand on the boy's shoulder as he hides behind him.

"Weese?" Bonko screws up his face.

"Reese," the kid answers.

"Aren't you somethin'?" Bonko reaches out and touches Reese's scraggly hair.

"Yours." Munroe pushes his son towards Bonko while Bailey weeps.

Bonko squints at the broken man.

Munroe forces his dangling jaw to hold together enough to make the offer. "Heard you like kids? Buy 'em? Yours." Munroe pushes the boy toward the diminutive, blood-splattered clown.

Watching Munroe offer up their child to Bonko makes Bailey snap.

"Stop! Don't! Not our son-"

"Your son," Munroe spits. "Who says the freak's mine?"

"Freak."

Bonko hears the words in a different voice; his father's. Spoken a thousand times. Said as he sits posing for a family photo with his other children, refusing to allow Bonko to join. Whispered in hushed arguments with his mother in the middle of the night. Spat in his face on the day his father finally disowned him, and then with defiance on the day Bonko came home...

"He's your son!" Bailey snarls.

"Could be anyone's." Munroe gargles.

"F-f-f-freak?" Bonko's lips hang on the word. "F-f-f-f-f-f-f-!" He screams, pushing past the boy, throwing him aside, and leaps on Munroe. The man barely has a second to react before Bonko starts wailing on his head with the right side of the hammer. Bone cracks, meat squishes, blood splatters, and the clown still keeps pounding.

He doesn't stop till he cracks a tile on the other side of mush and bone shards that was Munroe's head. The only thing left that resembles a face is half a jaw, missing some teeth.

Bailey's frozen in stunned horror, only reacting after Bonko rises covered in what's left of her boyfriend. She retches, hurling bile all over the tiles.

"Take him to Bruce." Bonko waves to the corpse, and two of his goons silently comply.

Reese sobs against the Coochie Trailer girl, her arms wrapped around his head to prevent him from seeing what's become of his father.

Bonko approaches Bailey, grip tight around the hammer. Her pleas for mercy are lost within despondent screeches.

"My pops had my mommy killed. He said he didn't, but he did. Blamed her for me, you see." Bonko squats and forces Bailey to look at him. "So I'm not gonna kill ya."

"N-no?" Bailey asks through mascara tears.

"No." Bonko strokes her cheek. "That'd be a damn waste now, wouldn't it. Pretty mommy like you?" A slow, cold smirk rises on his face. He holds it long enough for Bailey to click, to realize what he's got in store for her. Before she can protest, he orders, "take her to the Funhouse Trailer."

"No!" Bailey shrieks.

The image of that dilapidated trailer, a broken funhouse sign mounted on top, flashes before her eyes. Girls go in there, and so do men willing to pay a lot of money. Only one of them comes out.

"Please! No! Anything else! Please!" Perry stomps over, grabs Bailey by the hair, and drags her toward the door. "No!" She pulls free, tearing a clump of hair from her scalp and leaving behind a bloody patch.

Scrambling, Bailey makes a lunge and grabs a gun from one of the goons. She backs herself against the wall, flicking it from target to target.

"Watch where you're pointing that thing," Bonko warns. "You don't gots 'nuff bullets to shoot us all, Toots."

"How about just you?" She cocks the hammer and points it right at Bonko.

Without fear, he strides toward her, getting so close that the barrel pushes against his shiny red nose.

"Squeeze it." Bonko smirks. "I dare ya."

The gun shakes so much it honks Bonko's nose, and Bailey yelps. The girl holding Reese covers his ears. Everyone else in the room holds their breath.

"Boo!" Bonko laughs.

Bailey jumps.

She lowers the gun to her side, her arm shaking so bad it's liable to go off.

"Thought so." Bonko leers. "They're gonna love you back there; that's the toot-tootin'-"

Bailey shoves the gun in her mouth and pulls the trigger before Bonko can finish. A bloom of blood and brains spays across the wall, splattering inside the empty frame.

As Bailey's body slumps to the floor, Bonko steps over her and admires the fresh, dripping gore.

"This," he nods, "is art. Ay-yup!"

Bonko claps slowly, and his goons join in.

"Take her to Bruce too, but leave that." Bonko points to the frame. "It speaks to me."

He approaches the woman with Reese and nods to her. With an almost hidden pause of trepidation, she steps back and hands the boy over to Bonko. The clown takes the kid's hand and walks him out of the room as his goons get to work.

"I bet all the other kiddos make fun of you for that hair," Bonko says as they walk along a warped corridor.

"They," Reese sniffs, "call me monkey boy."

Bonko smirks. "You don't like that?"

"They're making fun of me. I'm not gonna see mommy and daddy again, am I?"

"No," Bonko stops and leans over so he's eye to eye with the kid. "Mommy and daddy did a bad thing. Now they've had to go away. But, tell ya what, kiddo, I can be your daddy now, ay-yup!"

"My daddy says I'm a freak."

That word makes Bonko want to break something else, but he holds the need for violence in check. For now.

"That what all the other boys and girls say too?"

"Uh-huh." Reese wipes away a tear.

"You wanna know what I say?"

Reese nods.

"That you, Reese." He boops the kid on the nose. "Are a monkey boy, and there's always a place at the carnival for a monkey boy."

"Y-you mean it?"

"Why sure! The carnival's a place for us f-f-f-folk's that don't belong nowhere else. Out there, this makes you a target." Bonko strokes the kid's whiskers. "In here makes you one of the f-f-f-family."

"Family?"

"Ay-yup! That's the toot-tootin' truth. In a bit, I'll introduce ya to your new sister."

"Sister? I always wanted a brother..."

"Yeah, well, them's the breaks, I guess. First, though, lemme see ya do a monkey dance."

Reese shuffles awkwardly, from foot to foot.

"No, you gotta do better, kiddo, or ain't no natives gonna pay a dime to see that dance."

Reese picks up the facade, throwing in some arm waves and whooping hips to better sell the act.

"Still not buyin' it." Bonko rubs his chin, smearing it with the blood of the kid's father. An idea hits him. "You know what would work?"

"Nu-huh." Reese stops and stares at the clown.

"Monkey's always got a hoppy limp thing goin' on." Bonko's hand finds its way to the hammer tucked into his belt as his eyes lock on Reese's foot.

"Y-you're not gonna hurt me, mister Bonko?"

"Kiddo." Bonko grips the hammer. "I'm about to make you a f-f-f-fuckin' star." He smiles so hard that he bites down on his lips, tasting Reese's parent's blood. "And that's the toot-tootin' truth."

Cut to: black.

Credits

As always, I have to thank Craig Walker and Casey Smallwood for braving the clowns and beta reading this short. Also, to Kyle Durrant, Sam Hallam, Cass Oakley, and Bret Laurie for their input.

A big thank you to Matt Taylor for the cover art.

About the Director

Christopher Robertson has been called the "Ryan Reynolds of Indie Horror" and "some Scottish Dr. Frankenstein." He doesn't care that they were joking. His stories are popcorn features that have been described as wholesome and gruesome in the same sentence multiple times. They include the 50s teen rom-zom-com *My Zombie Sweetheart*, kid-centric throwback *The October Society*, and 90s teen-comedy meta-slasher *Virgin Night*. You can find him on Instagram as @kit_romero, and he'd love it if you stalked him there.

Read More In

TERRORSCOPE STUDIOS PRESENTS:
THE COTTON CANDY MASSACRE
CHRISTOPHER ROBERTSON

THE COTTON CANDY MASSACRE

The book you are about to read is an account of the tragedy that occurred at the reopening of Bonkin's Bonanza one day in the summer of 1989.

Some came looking for fun, like Candy Barton and her best friend, Leigh. Others, like Rocky Rhodes and Sully Sullivan, came looking for a second chance. Instead, they would find a twisted, funfetti nightmare.

For many of the thrill-seekers and families visiting Bonkin's Bonanza, that day would be their last. And the events that unfolded would go on to become infamously known as ***THE COTTON CANDY MASSACRE***.

Once upon a time at a drive-in...

TERROR! From outer space comes crashing to Earth, giving rise to creatures of pure—

HORROR! The likes of which the quiet little town has never seen and the—

NIGHTMARE! That befalls two old friends as they struggle to survive against impossible odds!

It's Friday night, date night, in the quiet little town of Woodvale. For Suzie Palmer, this means hanging out at the All-Night Diner and maybe cruising up to Make-Out Point with her sweetheart. Little does she know there's something on its way to Woodvale. Something cruel and insidious. Something... out of this world...

MY ZOMBIE SWEETHEART is a love letter to 1950s sci-fi movies like *The Blob* and *Invasion of the Body Snatchers* It's a tale of young love and alien invaders coming soon to a drive-in near you!

Halloween approaches, and The October Society gathers.

They come to share their stories.

Tales of dark magic and crooked lies.

Of tragic pasts and wicked cruelty.

Of misguided misadventure and sinister pranks...

Collected here are the first six episodes of the spookiest show that never was. A series only found in the static between channels, that can only be watched on broken TVs in dusty attics and damp basements. Tune in, if you can, because the author of *MY ZOMBIE SWEETHEART* welcomes you to *THE OCTOBER SOCIETY*.

Before Valentine's Day, there is… *VIRGIN NIGHT*!

In the picturesque town of Cherry Lake, the kids aren't alright.

Neither is the centuries-old undead slasher that haunts the town.

Or the all-powerful megachurch with designs of the future.

On February 13th, 1998 — *VIRGIN NIGHT* — these will collide and the town of Cherry Lake will never be the same again.

For fans of self-aware 90s slashers — *VIRGIN NIGHT* will take you back to when low-rise jeans were cool, frosted tips were a thing, and getting laid was all that mattered.

Printed in Great Britain
by Amazon